HELLO KITTY®

Easter Bonnet Surprise

HELLO K. _ _ _ _

Easter Bonnet Surprise

Abrams Books for Young Readers, New York

It was Easter morning, and Hello Kitty and Mimmy were getting ready to go to the big Easter parade with all their friends in just a few hours.

Hello Kitty realized that she could not find the most important part of her outfit—her beautiful Easter bonnet! Hello Kitty asked Mimmy if she had seen it.

Mimmy suggested they look in Hello Kitty's room.
They looked under the bed, on the bookshelf,
and in the closet, but they could not find it.

Mimmy thought maybe the Easter bonnet was in her room, so they looked in Mimmy's room but could not find it.

Suddenly, Hello Kitty had an idea. If she went back to all the places she was yesterday when she last had it, maybe she would find it.

Hello Kitty and Mimmy began to retrace their steps.
They went to the park, where they ran into Tracy.
They explained that Hello Kitty's Easter bonnet was
missing, and that they needed it for the parade.

Maybe Hello Kitty left her Easter bonnet at school, where she had brought it for show-and-tell yesterday.

But the bonnet was not in the classroom or on the playground.
It wasn't on the school bus, either.

Hello Kitty, Mimmy, and Tracy checked the Lost and Found, but the bonnet wasn't there.

By now, Hello Kitty was worried that she would miss the parade. On their way home, Hello Kitty, Mimmy, and Tracy ran into Fifi, Joey, Rorry, and Thomas. Had they seen the Easter bonnet? None of them had.

Hello Kitty and her friends decided to stop at Grandma and Grandpa's house for some cookies. Grandpa was working on his garden.

Had Grandpa seen Hello Kitty's bonnet? No, he hadn't.
Hello Kitty was about to give up when she saw an old
wicker basket in Grandpa's garden and got an idea.
She could make a new Easter bonnet out of this basket,
just in time for the parade!

Fifi, Thomas, Tracy, Joey, Rorry, and Mimmy all helped to gather flowers and ribbon to make a new hat. They worked very hard to make the most beautiful Easter bonnet.

Hello Kitty and Mimmy put on their Easter bonnets and got to the parade just in time. Hello Kitty had the biggest and most beautiful Easter bonnet in the entire parade!

Hello Kitty's new Easter bonnet was very special because all of her friends had helped her make it. She would make sure never to lose it.

The Library of Congress has cataloged the 2004 edition
of this book as follows:

Library of Congress Cataloging-in-Publication Data
Hirashima, Jean.
Hello Kitty's Easter bonnet surprise / illustrated by Jean Hirashima.
p. cm.
Summary: When Hello Kitty loses her new Easter bonnet before the big parade,
Grandma White's old wicker basket provides a solution.
ISBN 0-8109-4819-2
[1. Hats—Fiction. 2. Easter—Fiction. 3. Lost and found possessions—Fiction.] I. Title.
PZ7.H3744534 2004
[E]—dc21
2003022142

ISBN for the 2013 edition: 978-1-4197-0910-4

Printed and bound in Mexico
10 9 8 7 6 5 4 3 2 1

Abrams Books for Young Readers are available at special discounts when purchased in quantity for premiums
and promotions as well as fundraising or educational use. Special editions can also be created to specification.
For details, contact specialsales@abramsbooks.com or the address below.

THE ART OF BOOKS SINCE 1949

**115 West 18th Street
New York, NY 10011
www.abramsbooks.com**